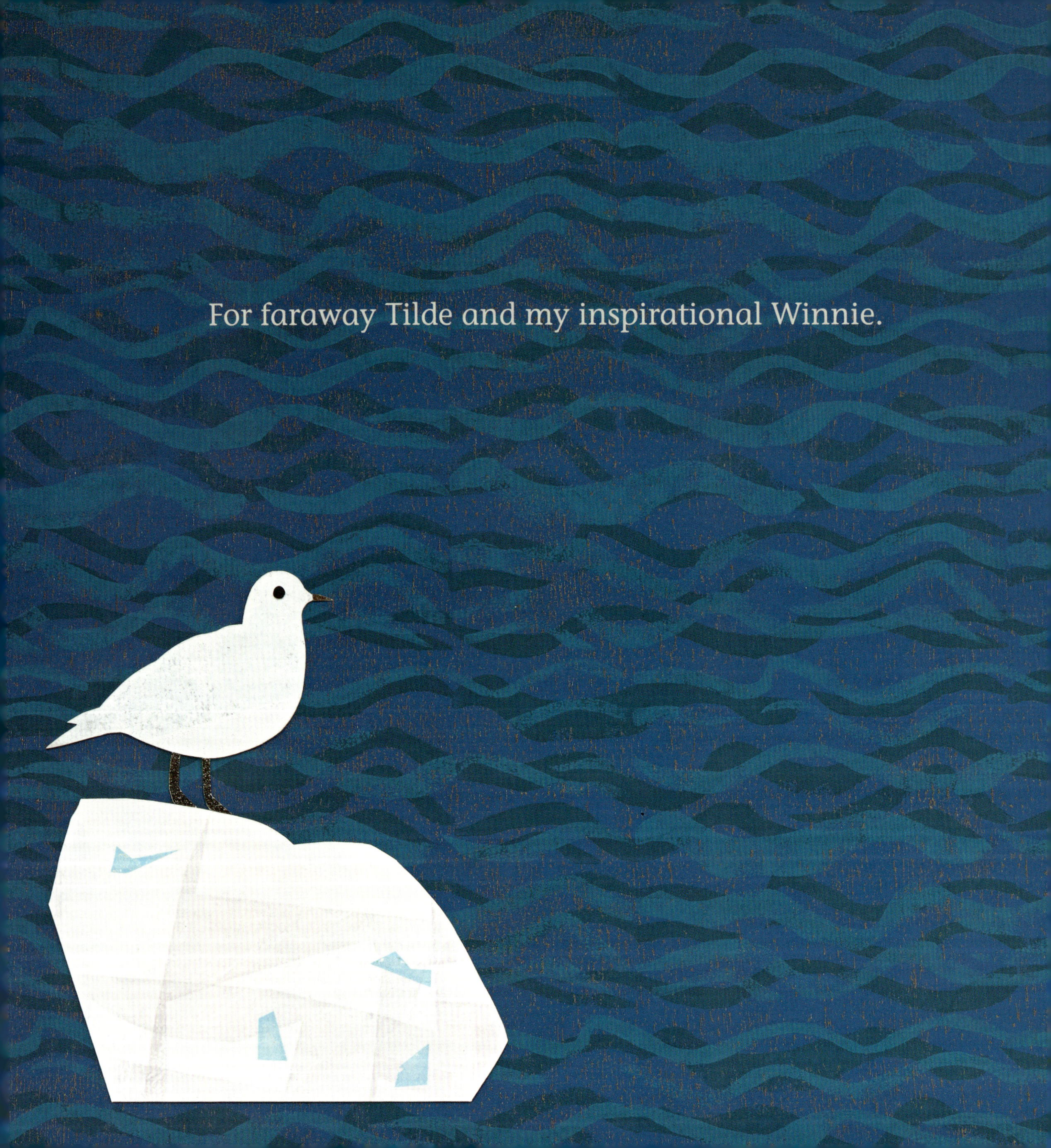

For faraway Tilde and my inspirational Winnie.

ANTARCTICA

MOIRA COURT

FREMANTLE PRESS

Antarctica is the coldest, windiest,

driest continent in the world.

It is an icy desert, with mountain ranges and sleeping volcanoes buried deep.

But it is also home to animals **amazing** and **unique**.

How many can you find?

One freckled, speckled leopard seal

sailing on an icy-blue berg.

Two courtly, portly emperor penguins

waddling across the polar plains.

Three lumbersome, cumbersome

elephant seals lining the sandy shore.

Four slow-paced, big-faced right whales

wallowing in rippling reflections.

Five speedy, beady-eyed snow petrels

somersaulting by craggy cliffs.

Six cheeky, sneaky orcas

surveying the frosty floe.

Seven inky, slinky flying squid

jetting around their watery world.

Eight shrimpish, pinkish Antarctic krill

drifting with the turning tide.

Nine nippy, slippy blackfin icefish

haunting the dusky depths.

Ten crimson, vermilion sea stars

creeping about on twinkle toes.

This diverse array of quirky creatures,

with their special fat or blood or feathers,

thrives at the very bottom of the world

in the harshest of all weathers.

DID YOU KNOW?

Antarctica is the southernmost continent in the world. It covers an area of 14 million square kilometres, nearly twice the size of Australia, and is almost completely covered in ice up to four kilometres thick. The average temperature during the coldest part of the year is –63°C, with the lowest temperature ever recorded a bone-chilling –89.2°C! Antarctica has hardly any rain or snow but it does have the windiest wind, with recorded speeds of up to 327 kilometres per hour.

The South Pole is in Antarctica, but there is more than one south pole: in fact, there are several!

There is the Geographical South Pole, which is the 'real' South Pole. It is the southernmost place in the world and is the end of the Earth's axis.

Nearby is the Ceremonial South Pole, a stout red-and-white striped pole, topped with a fancy, shiny metal ball.

There is also the Magnetic South Pole, which is where compasses point to when indicating south; the Geomagnetic South Pole, where the Earth's magnetic field begins; the Southern Pole of Inaccessibility, which is really, really, really, really hard to get to; and the Southern Pole of Cold, the coldest place on Earth.

Leopard seals are not only spotty like leopard cats, they are just as fierce. They prey on penguins and other smaller seals, catching them in their big mouths with long, sharp teeth. They are solitary animals who spend most of their lives alone.

Emperor penguins are the largest and toughest of all the penguins. They are the only animal to live on the open ice of Antarctica during the winter. Emperor penguins will walk 80 kilometres or more across the ice to feed in the open ocean.

Southern elephant seals are named after the males' inflatable snouts that resemble elephants' trunks. The largest of all seals, the male can be up to six metres long and weigh three tons — that's heavier than an ice-cream van! Despite being clumsy on land, southern elephant seals are excellent swimmers, able to stay underwater for two hours and reach depths of up to two kilometres.

Southern right whales are leisurely swimmers. They have white growths on their enormous heads called callosities. Callosities are home to whole colonies of whale barnacles, parasitic worms and whale lice.

Snow petrels are acrobatic aeronauts, swooping, soaring and plummeting at speeds of up to 40 kilometres per hour. They make their nests on ledges and in crevices of high cliffs and produce a stinky stomach oil that can be sprayed out of their mouths to keep trespassers away.

Orcas, or killer whales as they are also called, are the largest members of the dolphin family. They are among the most intelligent of all animals, being fast learners that are able to pass on their knowledge to other members of their pod, thus working as a team to hunt their prey. These crafty creatures use echolocation for navigation and hunting.

Flying squid when frightened squirt 'ink' from their bottoms, which spreads into a dark cloud that acts as a smokescreen. The squid then whizz safely away using jet propulsion.

Antarctic krill are six-centimetre-long crustaceans that live in huge swarms several kilometres wide. They have an exoskeleton, meaning their skeletons are on the outside of their bodies. They are on the menu for penguins, seals and whales.

Blackfin icefish are toothy, scaleless fish that produce a natural antifreeze in their bodies, which stops ice forming in their translucent blood. They live at the bottom of the ocean.

Sea stars, or starfish, have tube feet, eyespots at the end of each arm, two stomachs and a mouth in the middle of their underside with which they eat anything that they can find, including seal poo.

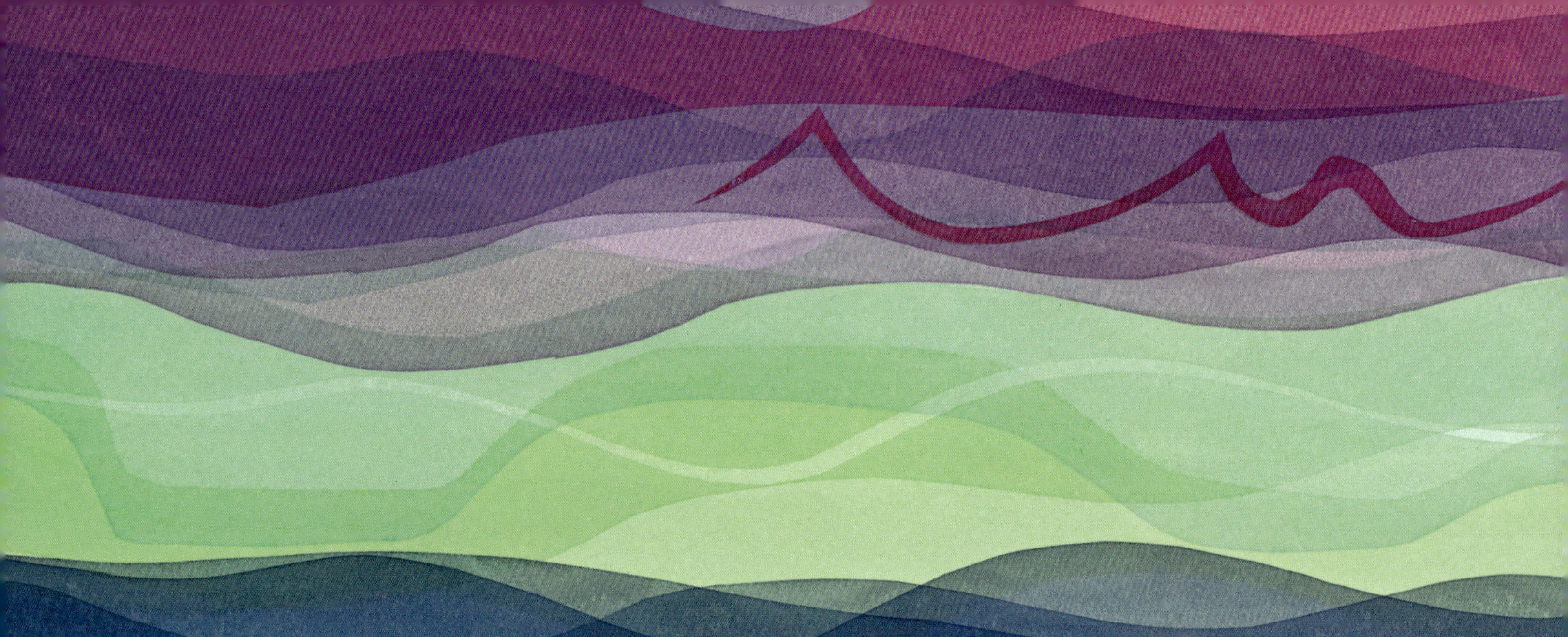

Moira Court is originally from the south-west of England but now lives in the Perth hills with her husband and daughter. Her work is inspired by nature, conservation, folklore and folk art. She has never been to Antarctica but really hopes to one day.
www.moiracourt.wordpress.com

First published 2019 by FREMANTLE PRESS
25 Quarry Street, Fremantle WA 6160
www.fremantlepress.com.au

Designed by Carolyn Brown (tendeersigh.com.au).
Printed by Everbest Printing Investment Limited, China.

Media: printmaking and collage.

National Library of Australia Cataloguing-in-publication data available.

ISBN: 9781925815757

Fremantle Press is supported by the State Government through the Department of Local Government, Sport and Cultural Industries.

Published with support from the Dorothy and Bill Irwin Charitable Trust